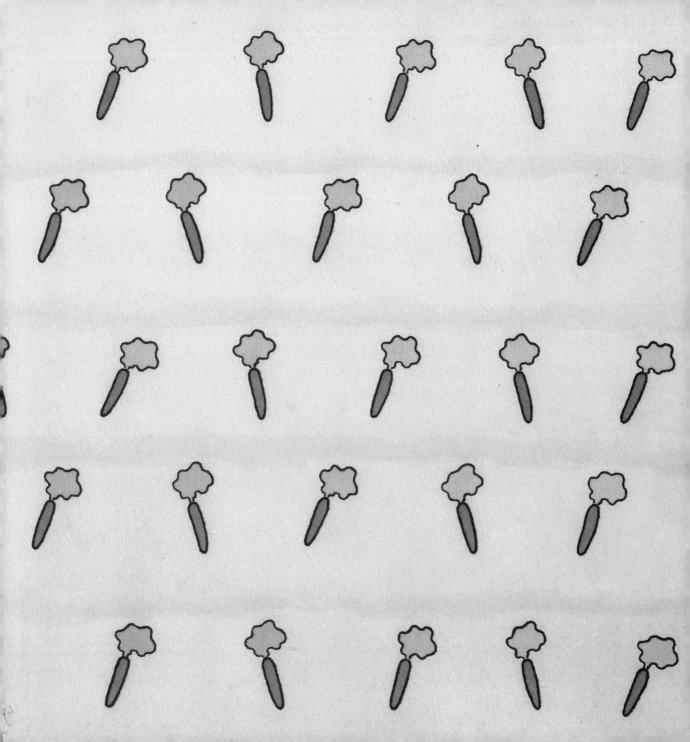

For Wendy,
who makes the very best costumes
B.R.M.

For Pam
S.L.

YOU DON'T GET A CARROT UNLESS YOU'RE A BUNNY

by BRIAN MANGAS

illustrated by Sidney Levitt

Simon and Schuster Books for Young Readers • Published by Simon & Schuster Inc., New York

The bunnies were getting ready for Halloween.
Honey Bunny was wearing a duck costume.
Sonny Bunny was wearing a bear costume.

They hopped to Owl's house.

Honey Bunny rang the doorbell.
Owl opened his door. "Who's there?" he asked.
"Trick or treat," said the bunnies.
"What?" said Owl.

"Pssst," Mrs. Owl whispered to Owl. "It's Halloween, dear."

She handed him a Halloween basket filled to the very top with good things for the little animals of the forest.

Owl reached inside and pulled out some Halloween treats.
"Here's some honey for you, Bear," he said. "And some duck
feed for you, little Duck. Happy Halloween."

The bunnies didn't say anything.

"What's the matter?" Owl asked.

"I think you gave us the wrong treats, Mr. Owl," Honey Bunny said. "May we have a carrot instead?"

"I'm sorry," Owl said. "I'm saving these carrots for the bunnies."

"We *are* the bunnies," Honey said.

"No, no," Owl said. "You're not bunnies. Bunnies don't have feathers and webbed feet. You're a duck. And you look like a bear to me," he said to Sonny.

"If you were bunnies, you would have big floppy ears,"
Owl said.

"Look, Mr. Owl," Sonny said.
He took off the furry brown earmuffs that Mother Rabbit
had used for his bear costume.

BRRWWAAAAANG... Two big bunny ears popped up.
Owl was startled and jumped back a bit.

"Well, you *do* have big ears, but that's not enough to make me believe you're a bunny," he said. "You could be a donkey or a baby elephant. They have big ears, too."

"Watch this, Mr. Owl," Honey Bunny said.
She kicked off the swim flippers that her mother had used
for webbed feet on her duck costume.

Then she shot high into the air with a giant bunny hop.
Sonny Bunny followed her, and they hopped all around Owl's tree.

"Now do you believe we're bunnies?" they asked.

"Maybe you are and maybe you're not," Owl said. "You could be frogs dressed as bunnies. Frogs hop, too, you know.

You'll have to do some more bunny things before I give you a carrot."

They twitched their bunny noses.
"Maybe," he said.

They wiggled their cottontails.
"Maybe," he said.

They thumped their big bunny feet.
"Maybe," he said.

They hopped and they flopped.
"I just don't know," said Owl.

Honey and Sonny didn't know what else to do. They
twitched their noses, thumped their feet, wiggled
their cottontails...

hopped and flopped until they dropped.

Owl put the basket down and called to his wife. By the time Mrs. Owl came to the door, the bunnies were gone.

"Do *you* think they were bunnies?" he asked her.

"They must have been bunnies," she said as she picked up
the basket. "They ate the carrots. And I don't blame them,"
she added. "All that hopping and flopping made them hungry."
   "Maybe," said Owl.

The End

SIMON AND SCHUSTER BOOKS FOR YOUNG READERS
Simon & Schuster Building, Rockefeller Center, 1230 Avenue of the Americas, New York, New York 10020.

SIMON AND SCHUSTER BOOKS FOR YOUNG READERS
is a trademark of Simon & Schuster Inc.
Manufactured in the United States of America.

10 9 8 7 6 5 4 3 2 1

Library of Congress Cataloging-in-Publication Data
Mangas, Brian. You don't get a carrot unless you're a bunny.
SUMMARY: Two bunnies dress up as a duck and a bear on Halloween,
but their trick backfires when they cannot get carrots
for their holiday treat. [1. Rabbits—Fiction.
2. Halloween—Fiction.] I. Levitt. Sidney, ill. II. Title. PZ7.M312644Yo 1989
ISBN 0-671-67201-0 88-19763

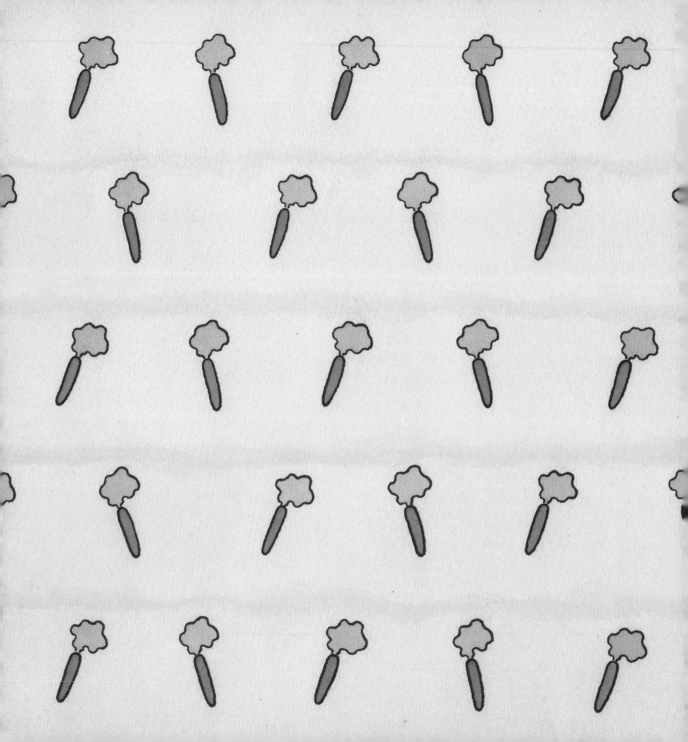